What's Going On Here?

The bathroom door was ajar. Oliver groaned. He pushed it open and looked inside.

There was Fang, stretched out in the bathtub. *But something was wrong!* Suddenly, Oliver's dog Pom-pom lunged forward and grabbed the alligator.

"Pom-pom! Cut that out!" shouted Oliver.

But Pom-pom wouldn't stop. He attacked Fang, snarling fiercely. The next thing Oliver knew, Pom-pom was tearing at the alligator with his teeth—and stuffing was coming out.

It wasn't Fang at all. It was just a stuffed alligator!

The real Fang was . . . missing!

OLIVER AND THE RUNAWAY ALLIGATOR

MICHAEL McBRIER

Illustrated by Blanche Sims

Troll Associates

Library of Congress Cataloging in Publication Data

McBrier, Michael.
    Oliver and the runaway alligator.

    Summary: Despite his mother's protests, Oliver
determines to care for a homeless baby alligator until
he can find its owner.
    [1. Alligators—Fiction. 2. Pets—Fiction]
I. Sims, Blanche, ill. II. Title.
PZ7.M47830m   1987   [Fic]   86-7120
ISBN 0-8167-0818-5 (lib. bdg.)
ISBN 0-8167-0819-3 (pbk.)

10   9   8   7   6   5   4   3   2   1

OLIVER AND THE RUNAWAY ALLIGATOR

CHAPTER
1

Oliver Moffitt watched Samantha Lawrence as she sent a stone skipping across the duck pond in Arrowhead Park. There weren't any ducks around—it was November. But it was a warm Friday afternoon, so lots of kids were at the pond.

"Two, three, four, five, six skips," Oliver counted. "That beats your record by one skip," he said to his friend Josh Burns.

"Can you beat it, Oliver?" Josh asked.

Oliver knew he could get seven skips if he threw just right. He was so busy winding up to throw that he didn't even notice Jennifer Hayes bounding down the path.

"Hi, guys!" she shouted. Oliver jumped. The

stone slipped out of his hand. *Plop!* It sank in the water—without a single skip!

"I can't stand how excited I am!" Jennifer went on, not noticing the dirty look Oliver gave her.

"Excited?" Samantha Lawrence got up from her seat on an old log. She was Oliver's next-door neighbor and best friend. "What's up?"

"Don't you *know*?" said Jennifer, putting her hands on her hips.

"It's Friday," said Matthew Farley. "No school for two days. No karate lessons, either." His parents were always sending him for some kind of special classes.

"I don't believe you guys!" Jennifer burst out. "You *really* don't know what today is?"

"National Computer Day?" Josh Burns asked. Josh loved computers.

"Wait a second, I've got it," Oliver said. "This is the anniversary of the day the Purple Worms bought their first guitars." Everybody laughed. Everybody except Jennifer. She was the Purple Worms' biggest fan. She bought all their records and covered the walls of her room with Purple Worms posters. Even her favorite color was purple. And she knew everything there was to know about the Purple Worms.

"Hey," said Sam, "I know what today is. This is the day the Worms' new video comes out."

"That's right!" cried Jennifer. "It'll be on TV after supper. Oh, I can't wait!"

"Is this the one called *Baby, I Love You, but Don't Get Too Close to Me*?" asked Sam.

"Yes," Jennifer replied. "*Oliver* ought to like it. The song is all about this guy and his pet alligator. And there's going to be a *real live alligator* in the video."

"No kidding," said Oliver. "Boy, wouldn't it be neat to have your own alligator?" Oliver didn't really care for the Purple Worms, but he loved animals. He was the only kid he knew who had his own pet-care business. Since he'd started, he'd taken care of everything from big dogs to monkeys.

"If you haven't seen the video yet, how do you know there's going to be an alligator in it?" Josh asked.

"Well, I read all the fan magazines," replied Jennifer. "And I *am* a member of the Purple Worms Fan Club—probably their most important member."

At that moment Oliver saw someone coming toward them. "Oh, no," he said.

"What is it?" asked Matthew.

"Here comes Rusty Jackson."

"Oh, no." Everybody groaned. Rusty was a big bully. He was also Oliver's number-one enemy.

"What do you think he's up to now?" whispered Sam.

"I don't know," Oliver replied, "but I'm afraid we're about to find out."

Rusty marched up to the group, carrying a big cardboard box.

"Hello, hello, hello, my friends," he said. "I suppose you know what today is."

"Well, of course we do," said Jennifer. She sounded offended. "It's the day the Worms' new video comes out."

"That's right," said Rusty. "And guess what I have right here?" He pointed to the box and smiled his sinister smile. He sat down and opened it up.

Jennifer gasped as Rusty pulled out a sequin-studded purple T-shirt with an alligator on the front. Then he pulled out stickers with pictures of the Purple Worms on them. Then he pulled out a purple barrette shaped like an alligator, and a purple mug that said "Purple Worms" on it, and a purple pencil.

Oliver leaned forward to look inside the box. There were several of each of the things Rusty had shown them. "Where did you get all this stuff?" asked Oliver.

"It's my new business," replied Rusty proudly. "I'm a Purple Worms souvenir salesman. I sell this stuff for the M and R Novelty Company."

Oliver looked doubtful.

Rusty narrowed his eyes. "Want to make something of it?" he snarled.

"No, no," said Oliver quickly.

"I really want to buy something," said Jennifer, "but all I've got is fifty cents."

Rusty snorted. "Can't get much for that," he said. "Just one of these rings." He slipped a purple plastic ring onto his finger. There was a picture of the Worms' lead singer on it. When Rusty tilted the ring, the picture changed to an alligator.

"Wow!" exclaimed Jennifer. "I'll take one!"

"Me too!" said Sam.

Oliver glared at Sam. "Well, I like them," she said, shrugging.

By this time even Josh and Matthew looked interested. Oliver didn't say a word as they handed Rusty money for Purple Worms rings.

"Boy, am I going to rake in the dough," said Rusty. "Hey, what about you, Moffitt? Aren't you going to buy one?"

"No way," said Oliver. "I wouldn't—" He stopped speaking. "Did you hear something?" he whispered.

"Probably just a dumb squirrel," replied Rusty. "I think you should buy one of these . . . AAAAAH!" he screamed. "A monster!"

Over the top of the cardboard box a pair of shiny black eyes and a long scaly face peeked at Rusty. The creature was slender, less than two feet long, and black with yellow bands.

"That's no monster," said Oliver, staring at the pointed nose and long tail. "It's an alligator! A baby alligator!"

Sam, Matthew, Josh, Jennifer, and Rusty crowded around.

"Wow!"

"Gosh!"

"Where'd he come from?"

Oliver stooped to examine the alligator. But he didn't get too close. He was sure there were a lot of teeth inside its mouth. "What are you doing out here, little fella?" he asked it. "I thought you guys lived in places where it's warm. Isn't this too cold for you?"

"Maybe he belongs to the Purple Worms!" Jennifer cried.

"Not likely," said Oliver. "He must be somebody's pet. And he must be lost. He needs to be somewhere warm."

"What should we do?" asked Sam.

"Look for his owner," Josh suggested.

"Maybe later. But right now I'm going to take him home. He's got to warm up."

"How do you know it's a *he*?" asked Jennifer.

"I don't," answered Oliver. "He just looks like one." Oliver reached toward the little alligator. Just then Rusty's foot came down—right in front of Oliver's hand. The alligator jumped. "Hey!" cried Oliver.

"Just a minute," said Rusty. "You don't see many pets like this around here. I'll bet it's valuable. You can't just take it. We could sell it to a pet store and make a lot of money."

"No way," said Oliver.

"Who made you the boss of the alligator?" asked Rusty, his hands on his hips.

Oliver stood up and faced him. "No one. But you're not the boss, either."

"Come on! We can *all* make money," Rusty insisted.

Oliver looked at his friends. "Let's take a vote," he said. "How many want to sell this innocent baby alligator—"

"—and split all the money we'd get," added Rusty. He raised his hand. No one else did.

"I should have guessed," said Rusty. He made a grab for the alligator.

SNAP! The alligator's jaws opened and closed in a flash, showing rows of sharp white teeth.

"He almost bit me!" yelled Rusty, scrambling to his feet.

"It looks like he knows an enemy when he sees one," said Matthew.

Meanwhile, the alligator had turned back to Rusty's box. It reached up to one of the cardboard flaps and started chewing on it.

"Hey!" shouted Rusty. "Let go of that!" He grabbed the other side of the box—farthest from those sharp teeth—and tried to pull it away. The alligator didn't budge. All Rusty managed to do was tear the box. Purple Worms souvenirs scattered all over the ground.

"Get him away from my things!" Rusty was jumping around in excitement. "If he ruins any of my merchandise, I . . . I . . ." A crafty look suddenly came over his face. "I'll sell him to cover the damage he causes."

Oliver knelt down as the alligator nosed around in Rusty's stuff. "Come here, little fella." He gently turned the alligator away from the souvenirs. The alligator blinked its eyes. "You should have a name," Oliver said.

"What about Fang?" suggested Sam. "He has such nice teeth."

"Oh, that's good," said Oliver.

"All your stuff is fine, Rusty," Josh said, putting the souvenirs back into the box. "All except this." He held up one of the Purple Worms rings. Fang had left tooth marks all over it.

"It's ruined!" Rusty said. "No one will ever buy a chewed-up thing like that. There's only one thing to do—sell that overgrown lizard and hope I get enough money to—"

"Hold it," said Oliver. "That's just a fifty-cent ring. You're not going to trade Fang for *that*."

"Then how will I get my fifty cents back?" Rusty demanded.

Oliver dug into his pocket. Out came a quarter, two dimes, and a nickel. "Here. Now I'm taking Fang home."

"Do you want your ring?" said Rusty.

"Keep the dumb thing!" Oliver replied.

"Wow!" said Jennifer. "This is incredible! Now we have a real alligator, just like in the Purple Worms' video!" She grabbed Oliver's arm. "Couldn't *I* keep him? Then I could pretend I'm one of the Worms."

"It's not easy to take care of an alligator," said Oliver. "And your mother probably wouldn't like having one in the house. Besides, I'm a pet-care expert. I know how to handle things like this."

"Well . . . all right," Jennifer said. Oliver picked up Fang and tried to tuck him into his pocket, but he wouldn't fit. He kept wriggling around. Oliver put him underneath his jacket. Finally Fang settled down.

"Let's go," said Oliver to his friends.

Rusty looked up from his torn carton of

Purple Worms souvenirs. "I'll get you back for this, Moffitt!" he shouted as Oliver and his friends walked away.

Oliver ignored him.

"What are you going to do with Fang now?" Sam asked.

"Oh, no problem," Oliver replied. "I'll think of something." But Oliver knew that taking care of an alligator was not going to be an easy job.

CHAPTER
2

"Soon you'll be nice and warm," Oliver told Fang as he walked up the path to his front door.

"Hullo," said a small voice.

Sitting on the Moffitts' steps was Kelly Helfman. Kelly lived five doors down the street. She was only six years old.

"I rang your bell," said Kelly, "but no one answered."

"My mom's still at work," Oliver told her. Mrs. Moffitt worked for an insurance agency in town. She usually got home just before six.

"Oh," said Kelly.

"So, what's up?" asked Oliver, glancing at

Fang. The little alligator was probably freezing by now.

Kelly held out her hand to Oliver. "I have twenty-seven cents," she said, showing him a quarter and two pennies. "I need a pet-sitter for the weekend. We're taking a trip to my grandma's house."

"Oh," said Oliver. "What kind of pet do you have?"

Kelly reached behind her back and pulled out a mayonnaise jar with holes punched in the lid. "I have a bug," she told Oliver. "His name is Mr. Brown."

Oliver bent over to peer into the jar. All he could see was grass and twigs.

"I don't know what kind of bug he is," said Kelly, "but I need you to take care of him."

"Why don't you just let him go?" suggested Oliver. "That way Mr. Brown could be free, and you wouldn't have to pay me twenty-seven cents. Then you could find another bug when you come back." Oliver knew that bugs in jars usually didn't last very long. He knew Mr. Brown probably wouldn't be alive by the time the weekend was over. He didn't want Kelly to be upset. And he didn't want any of the pets he took care of to die.

"No," said Kelly. "I don't want to let him go. I need you to take care of him. Please."

Oliver chewed his lip. "Why don't you take Mr. Brown with you?" he asked. "He might like a vacation too."

"I can't bring him with me," said Kelly. "My grandma hates bugs."

Oliver sat down beside Kelly. He looked into the jar again. This time he saw Mr. Brown, a shiny beetle, crawling up a stalk of grass.

"Please," said Kelly, "you're a pet-sitter. You *have* to take him." Kelly's voice quavered as if she might cry.

"Okay, okay," said Oliver quickly.

"Is twenty-seven cents enough?" asked Kelly.

"It's fine," replied Oliver. "When will you be back?"

Before Kelly could answer, Fang began squirming around under his jacket. "Yikes!" cried Oliver. He jumped up and pulled Fang out. "Okay, okay. I'd better get you inside. You come too, Kelly."

Oliver unlocked the front door and went inside.

"What's that thing?" asked Kelly, following Oliver.

"A baby alligator," he answered. "I found him near the pond."

Oliver closed the door. He stood in the middle of the living room holding the squirming baby alligator, trying to figure out what to do with him. At that moment Pom-pom, Mrs. Moffitt's frisky little Shih Tzu, came running to greet him. Pom-pom stopped short when he saw Fang.

Fang opened his mouth in a toothy smile.

Pom-pom took one look, tucked his tail between his legs, and ran off.

"Oliver?" said a voice behind him.

"Mom!" Oliver whirled around. "I didn't hear you come home."

"How was your day, d—*aughhh!* Oliver, what is *that*? Get it out of the house this instant!" Mrs. Moffitt clutched at her briefcase and a small bag of groceries.

At that moment Fang wriggled out of Oliver's grasp and landed on the floor with a plop. He darted under the couch.

Mrs. Moffitt ran halfway up the stairs. "Where is it? Where is it?" she screamed. "Oliver, find that thing!"

Oliver got down on his hands and knees and looked under the sofa. Kelly joined him.

No Fang.

He looked under the chairs.

No Fang.

Kelly looked behind the drapes.

No Fang.

"Oliver . . ." Mrs. Moffitt warned.

"I know, I know."

"Where's Pom-pom?" she exclaimed.

"Hiding," Oliver replied. "I think he's safe."

Fang poked his head out from under a chest of drawers and crawled out onto the carpet.

"There he is!" cried Kelly. She and Oliver charged after Fang, but the alligator was fast. Before they could get him, he'd zipped under the sofa.

"Get around the other side!" Oliver told Kelly. "It's okay now, Mom. We've got him surrounded."

But Fang wasn't ready to give up. He ran out from under the sofa. Oliver grabbed for him, and missed. Fang darted for the kitchen.

"I'll get him!" Kelly made a flying leap for the little alligator and caught him just as he was about to run behind the refrigerator. She handed him proudly to Oliver.

"Thanks," said Oliver. He cradled Fang in his arms and carried him back to the living room.

"Look, Mom," said Oliver. "He's a very gentle alligator." Oliver ran his finger down Fang's back. "And he's pretty."

"He's *still* an alligator," said Mrs. Moffitt with a shudder.

"But he's just a baby," Oliver added. "Look at his teeth. See his nice smile?"

Fang opened his mouth and showed off his teeth.

"Okay. That's enough. I want him out of the house immediately. Take him back where he belongs."

"But that's the problem, Mom," said Oliver. "He doesn't belong anywhere. I found him in the park. He's lost."

"So what do you plan to do?"

"Take care of him until I find his owner."

Mrs. Moffitt set her mouth in a straight line. "No."

"Please, Mom? Please?"

"Oliver." Mrs. Moffitt sat down on the arm of a chair. "It's not going to be easy to find his owner. It may take a very long time."

"But Mom, how many lost alligators could there be? The owner will probably report it right away. I'll bet finding the owner will be easy."

"Oliver, NO. No alligators in the house. I've had to put up with dogs and cats and all sorts of animals that don't belong to you. But I draw the line at an alligator. . . . No."

"Mom, didn't you once say that we should be nice to those less fortunate than ourselves?"

"*People*, Oliver, people."

Oliver sighed. "But if I put him back outside, I think he'll die, Mom."

"Die?"

"Yes. Really. He's a cold-blooded animal. He needs warmth."

"Fine. Take him to a nice, warm pet store."

"No! They'd sell him. Then his owner would never get him back. How would you like it if Pom-pom were lost and someone found him and—"

"Okay, okay."

"Can I keep him?"

"Absolutely not."

"I mean, can I take care of him while I look for his owner?"

"Well, where would you put . . . Fang while you search for his owner?"

"I was just thinking about that," said Oliver. "I'll be right back." Holding Fang, Oliver dashed upstairs. Kelly was at his heels. Oliver looked into his room, which was also the office for his pet-sitting business, but he didn't see anyplace that would be good for Fang. Then Oliver saw it—his mother's bathroom. The perfect place for an alligator.

If Fang splashed water, he wouldn't ruin anything.

If he made a mess, it would be easy to clean up.

It was better than his own bathroom, because the tub was larger. Fang would have more room to exercise. And since his mother's shower was broken, she had to use Oliver's tub anyway.

Oliver filled the tub with six inches of warm water and placed the alligator into it. Fang swam briskly from one end of the tub to the other, grinning and showing off his teeth.

"That looks like a good place for him," said Kelly.

Oliver nodded his head. "Now," he told Fang, "you stay right there and be good."

Oliver closed the door. Then he opened it again. He bent down, rolled up the bath mat, and put it on a shelf in the linen closet—just in case. If Fang *did* climb out of the tub, Oliver didn't want him chewing anything up.

Oliver closed the door again. Then he opened it again. This time he took the soap, scrub brush, and toothbrushes and put *them* in the linen closet too—just in case.

Oliver looked into the tub and smiled. There was Fang, lolling in the water with his eyes half closed!

Kelly laughed. "He's happy," she said.

Oliver sighed. He shut the door and ran back

downstairs. "Okay, Mom," he announced. "The problem is solved."

"All right," said Mrs. Moffitt. "Where is he?"

"In the bathtub."

Mrs. Moffitt nodded her head. "Do you understand that this is a *temporary* arrangement? That he can stay here only until you find his owner or a new owner?"

"Yes, Mom. I understand," Oliver said. "And Mom—thanks!"

Mrs. Moffitt smiled faintly. "Now, it's almost dinnertime," she said. "Has that little thing had any food?"

"Not yet. Alligators are meat eaters," said Oliver thoughtfully, "but I'm not sure what to feed him."

"There's chicken in the refrigerator. I was going to cook it for dinner. We could give some to Fang."

"I don't know, Mom. He's so little."

"His teeth are certainly in fine shape," Mrs. Moffitt said.

"Well, I'm going to give him something easier to eat the first time around. Maybe he'd like Pom-pom's food." Oliver took a can of Beef 'n' Liver Dinner from the cupboard.

"By the way, where *is* Pom-pom?" asked his mother.

Before Oliver could answer, he heard a faint scratching sound. Pom-pom stepped out of a cupboard beneath the sink.

"Pom-pom!" cried Mrs. Moffitt. "You poor

baby! Did Fang scare you?" She picked up the little dog and held him in her arms.

The doorbell rang. It was Sam. "We're almost ready to eat dinner, but Mom said I could come over to see how Fang's doing," she said.

"He's in the bathtub now," Oliver told her. "I'm just about to give him his dinner. Want to help me?"

"Sure," replied Sam.

Oliver and Sam went back to the kitchen. Oliver spooned some Beef 'n' Liver Dinner into an aluminum pie plate. Then he and Sam dashed upstairs.

"Oliver?"

"Kelly?" Oliver had almost forgotten about her in all the excitement. He turned to see her at the bottom of the stairs.

"I have to go now," she said. "What about Mr. Brown?"

"Are you sure you want me to take him?"

"Yes," replied Kelly. "Here's the money." She put the jar and the coins on a table. "We'll be back on Monday afternoon."

"No problem."

"Take good care of him."

"I will," said Oliver, but he felt as if there were a stone in the pit of his stomach. "See you, Kelly. Have fun."

"Good-bye, Mr. Brown," said Kelly. Two tears ran down her cheeks.

"Gosh," said Oliver after she'd left. "She sure likes that bug."

"Yeah," said Sam. "Hey! I'll bet Fang's food

will float in the tub. Pretty neat, huh? Floating food."

"Yeah," said Oliver. "Now let's see if he'll eat it."

CHAPTER
3

Oliver and Sam took the pie plate with the Beef 'n' Liver Dinner into the bathroom. Oliver closed the door.

"There he is," he told Sam, pointing into the bathtub.

"I don't believe this," said Sam.

"What?"

"Your mother let you keep Fang in her bathtub?"

"Well, she didn't seem to mind when I told her. Besides, he has more room in here."

"Oh," said Sam uncertainly.

Fang was swimming around lazily.

Oliver placed the pie plate on the water. Sure enough, it floated.

"Come on, Fang," said Oliver. He tapped the plate.

Fang swam over to see what it was. But as he tried to sniff the food, the plate floated away. Fang swam to it again. This time the plate bumped into the side of the bathtub and went off in another direction.

"Well, this isn't going to work," said Oliver. "We'll have to take him out of the tub."

"Okay," replied Sam. "Where's the bath mat?"

"In the linen closet. Here, put this old towel down instead."

Oliver and Sam spread out a ragged towel that Mrs. Moffitt used for drying Pom-pom when he got caught in the rain. Then Oliver lifted Fang out of the water. "Now try it," he said.

Fang stuck his snout into the dish. Then he opened his mouth and took a big bite.

"I think he likes it!" said Oliver.

Fang took another bite . . . and another . . . and another. Then he stopped and wandered toward the linen closet. Oliver closed the door before Fang went inside.

"Well?" said Sam.

"I don't know," said Oliver. "He took only three bites of his dinner."

"Maybe he's not hungry," said Sam. "Maybe he hasn't been lost for very long, or maybe he found things to eat at the pond."

"Or maybe he just doesn't like dog food," said Oliver. "I wouldn't." He scooped up Fang and put him back into the tub. "I'd better look up alligators in my pet encyclopedia."

*   *   *

After dinner Oliver went to his room. He took the encyclopedia from his shelf and sat down on his bed. Chapter Seven was called "Reptiles as Pets" and had lots of stuff about alligators.

The most interesting thing Oliver learned was that Fang might be something called a caiman, not an alligator, since baby caimans are generally what people buy or give as pets. A true baby alligator would be a very rare pet. Whatever Fang was, though, he was not going to be easy to feed.

The book said that alligators and caimans are picky eaters and that at first they might refuse everything. Dog food would be okay, but Oliver should try giving Fang minnows, worms, insects, and small pieces of fish, liver, and raw meat.

The most important thing Oliver learned was that Fang's water should be kept somewhere between 80 and 95 degrees, which was pretty warm. Oliver found a thermometer and tied it to a string so that he could hang it from the faucet in the tub. That way he could keep an eye on the water temperature.

The next thing the book mentioned was going to be even harder. It said that baby caimans need to get *completely* dry after they've been in the water. In the wild they do this by basking in the sun, but sitting under a sun lamp would do almost as well. "Oh, boy," thought Oliver.

Oliver also realized that he should put something into the tub to help Fang get out of the water once in a while. The book suggested a low ramp that sloped into the water, but Oliver didn't have anything like that.

Searching around in his room, he found an old wooden block and some bricks he'd taken from a vacant lot. A long loud scream rang through the house.

Oliver dropped the block with a clatter. He flew out of his room. "Mom?" he called. "Mom? Mom!"

Mrs. Moffitt came barreling out of her bathroom dressed in her robe. She left the door open behind her.

"Uh-oh," said Oliver.

Mrs. Moffitt leaned against the wall.

"Fang?" asked Oliver.

"Young man," began his mother, "all I wanted was a long hot bath. I had a very hard day today. I needed to unwind. And what do I find when I start to run the water? *That*," she said, pointing at Fang, who blinked his eyes innocently. "I almost stepped into the tub with him."

"But Mom," said Oliver, "I *told* you I put him in the tub."

"I thought you meant *your* tub."

"Oh. But I put him in your tub because it's bigger—and you've been using *my* tub."

Mrs. Moffitt sighed. "I can't brush my teeth with an alligator watching me. You'll have to move Fang into your bathroom."

"Okay, Mom. Thanks."

"One more thing, Oliver. I'm going to put a time limit on this temporary arrangement. You

may have one week to find an owner for Fang. That's all."

"One week?"

"Don't press your luck."

"Okay, okay. No problem. Fang won't be any trouble at all. You'll see."

Mrs. Moffitt went downstairs, shaking her head.

Oliver moved Fang into his bathtub. Then he went to his room and got the wooden block. He put it at one end of the bathtub, resting on the bricks. The top was just an inch above the level of the water, and the bricks made a stairway so Fang could climb up. "Pretty good!" said Oliver.

He hung the thermometer in the water. Seventy-five degrees. Not warm enough. Oliver added some hot water. Then he showed Fang the block. "Look," he said. "Now you can sit up here and get out of the water. You can pretend you're sunning yourself."

Fang swam over to the block and climbed up. He looked at Oliver. He opened his mouth in a grin. Oliver patted his scaly back. "I don't know why Mom doesn't like you," he said. "But don't worry, I do. Now I'm going to make a phone call and find out what to do about a sun lamp for you."

Oliver left Fang grinning away in the bathtub. He went to his office and looked at a list of phone numbers. When he found the one he needed, he picked up the telephone and dialed Mr. Whitman. Mr. Whitman was Oliver's all-time favorite teacher.

Oliver knew that he was working on a special

science experiment. Mr. Whitman had turned the whole first floor of his house into a climate-controlled environment for reptiles and amphibians. He was caring for lizards, toads, snakes, alligators, and more.

A booming voice answered the phone. "HEL-LO?" Oliver could just picture Mr. Whitman. With his bulging stomach and long white beard, he looked a little like Santa Claus without the red suit.

"Hello, Mr. Whitman. It's Oliver Moffitt."

"OLIVER! It's good to hear from you. How are you?"

Oliver held the phone away from his ear. "I'm fine, but I need some information. I found a lost baby caiman today. Well, actually he might be an alligator. Anyway, I'm taking care of him until I can track down his owner."

"THAT'S A TALL ORDER. Do you have a sun lamp?"

"That's why I was calling," said Oliver.

Mr. Whitman told Oliver about a pet shop where he could rent a sun lamp.

Oliver hung up feeling satisfied. It was good to know he could turn to his teacher for help with Fang. Tomorrow he would get the sun lamp. But right now he needed to check on Mr. Brown. Oliver looked into the jar, which was sitting on his desk.

"Hello there, Mr. B.," said Oliver cheerfully. "How are you doing?"

It took Oliver a moment to see the bug among all the grass and twigs. When Oliver did find him, he thought he looked a little sluggish. Oliver felt that stone in his stomach again. He remembered the tears rolling down Kelly's cheeks when she'd said good-bye to her friend. Then he thought of his reputation as a pet-care expert.

"Come on, Mr. Brown," he said encouragingly. "You've got to last until Monday afternoon, okay?"

Oliver sprinkled a few drops of water into the jar so Mr. Brown would have enough moisture. He was just replacing the lid when he heard a thump.

Oliver raced down the hall. The door to his bathroom was open! He must have forgotten to close it. He hardly dared to peek inside and see what had happened.

Splash!

Oliver burst into the bathroom.

Water was everywhere. It had sloshed out of the tub, run along the floor, and splashed on the walls. In the tub were Fang—and Pom-pom!

"Pom-pom!" Oliver cried.

Oliver slammed the door shut and reached into the bathtub. Fang, his teeth bared, had cornered Pom-pom, who was yipping, dripping, and slipping, trying to get out of the bathtub.

Oliver dived for Fang, but tripped. *Splosh!* He fell into the tub. He shook water from his eyes and grabbed the alligator. "Okay, Pom-pom," Oliver said, "get out. Get out *now*."

Pom-pom scrambled to the edge of the tub. Then he slid back into the water.

"Oh, no! Your paws are slippery. Try again."

Whoosh! Pom-pom tried again, but slid all the way to the other end of the tub.

"Oh, brother," said Oliver. "I'll have to help."

Oliver stood up, still holding Fang. "I'll put you down on your block, and then give Pom-pom a hand."

He took one sloshy step toward the wooden block—and his foot landed on a bar of soap. Oliver's feet slipped out from under him. He landed on his seat in the middle of the tub. The alligator flew out of his hands and landed on the floor—just as Pom-pom managed a flying leap out of the tub.

Pom-pom found himself face-to-face with Fang. He managed one terrified yelp as the baby caiman opened his mouth wide and drew back. Pom-pom turned around to run, but saw *another* Fang in the mirror behind him. With a howl the dog leaped back into the bathtub.

Oliver was just wiping the water from his eyes, when his mother opened the door. "Oliver!" she gasped. "What happened? How did that alligator get *out* of the tub, and why are you and Pom-pom *in* it?" She backed away from Fang.

Oliver lifted Pom-pom out of the tub and handed him to Mrs. Moffitt. He reached for Fang and gently set him on the wooden block.

Mrs. Moffitt hugged Pom-pom. "You're soaking wet," she said, reaching for a towel, "and you're *bleeding*! Oliver, he's bleeding!"

Oliver stepped out of the bathtub, his sneakers squishing. He looked where his mother was pointing. Sure enough, on Pom-pom's left front paw were several drops of blood. "Uh-oh," said Oliver. "I guess Fang, um, bit him."

"Well," said Mrs. Moffitt. "That does it!"

"But Mom, Pom-pom must have scared Fang. He was just defending himself."

"Oliver, Fang is dangerous. Tomorrow you'll have to take him to the pet store."

"Please, Mom, no!"

"I mean it. The next thing you know, he'll be biting one of us. I won't have that." Mrs. Moffitt was drying Pom-pom briskly. Oliver could tell she was angry.

"It was my fault. I didn't close the door tightly."

"And I suppose you stood here and made Fang bite Pom-pom too?"

"Well, no."

Mrs. Moffitt put on her "I thought so" look.

"What if I got a muzzle for Fang?" he said. "Then he couldn't bite." Mrs. Moffitt dried Pom-pom's ears. She dabbed at his cut with a tissue.

"You did say I could look after him," Oliver went on.

"Yes, I did. But that was before Fang had bitten anything."

"If I get him a muzzle, he won't be able to bite."

Mrs. Moffitt put Pom-pom out in the hall. "All right," she said finally. "But only if he wears a muzzle. And I want him wearing it anytime he's not eating. Do you understand me?"

"Then Fang can stay?" asked Oliver. "I mean, just for the week?"

"Yes," said his mother. "For the week."

"Thanks," said Oliver. "I'll buy a muzzle at the pet store." He would have to go there to rent the sun lamp anyway. And he could ask about buying minnows and earthworms.

Oliver wanted Fang to be as comfortable as possible for the week he'd be staying in the Moffitt home. "One week!" thought Oliver. "How will I ever find Fang's owner in just one week?"

CHAPTER
4

On Saturday Oliver woke up early. He got out of bed and walked right over to the jar on his desk to check on Mr. Brown. The bug was still alive. So far so good. Oliver sprinkled some water into the jar. Later he would add a few blades of grass.

Next Oliver peeped into the bathroom. He was worried about the mess he might find. But the bathroom was neat. Fang was spread out on the block sleeping. Oliver looked at the thermometer in the water. It read 75 degrees, so he drained the tub slightly and added hot water. He also turned the heat up in the room.

After Oliver had given Fang another plate of dog food and eaten his own breakfast, it was time to go to the pet store. He took all the money he had earned from pet-sitting and stuffed it into his pockets.

"I'm going to the pet store!" Oliver called to his mother as he headed out the front door. "Be back soon."

At the pet store Oliver looked at the dog muzzles. They came in all sizes. "May I help you, young man?"

Oliver turned to face one of the store clerks. "Yes, please," he replied. "I need a muzzle. It's for an . . . it's for a small . . . dog. A very small dog."

"Sure thing," said the clerk. He reached behind a counter and handed Oliver a tiny muzzle. It looked perfect.

Next Oliver asked about minnows, live insects, and other special foods for Fang. Then he rented a sun lamp for a week.

When Oliver had paid for everything, he had only two dollars and twelve cents left. Boy, he thought, Fang is costing me a lot of money, and he isn't even a client.

Back home Oliver had to struggle with Fang's snapping jaws for several seconds before the muzzle was on properly. It seemed a little loose, but Oliver thought it would do the trick. Oliver looked sadly at Fang, who looked sadly back at him.

"I'm really sorry," he told the little alligator.

Mrs. Moffitt appeared in the doorway to the bathroom. "That's much better," she said.

Oliver nodded.

He rigged up the sun lamp and let Fang sample some of his new food.

When Fang was all set, Oliver found Pom-pom and picked him up, nuzzling his face. "Come on, Pom-pom," he said. "We've got work to do. Let's get everyone to help us."

Oliver clipped Pom-pom's leash to his collar and walked him next door to Sam's house. Sam and Jennifer answered the bell together. "Did you see the video last night?" asked Jennifer. "It was great!"

"No, I missed it," said Oliver.

Jennifer looked astonished. "*Missed* it! I don't see how— "

"Hey, how's Fang?" Sam asked.

"He's fine," said Oliver. "Do you want to help me look for his owner?"

"Sure!" said Sam.

"Good. Let's go get Matthew and Josh."

Jennifer didn't look too eager, but she came along anyway.

A little while later Oliver rang Matthew's doorbell, prepared for a long wait on the porch. He figured it might take a while to tear Matthew away from whatever he was doing. Matthew was usually practicing one of his lessons.

When Matthew finally answered the door, Oliver asked, "Want to help us look for Fang's owner?"

"Sure. I'm supposed to be building a model of a space shuttle for my rocketry class, but I guess that can wait."

"Okay. Let's go get Josh."

"That won't be necessary."

Everyone whirled around. There was Josh, standing behind them.

"Hey!" exclaimed Oliver. "Why aren't you home working on your computer?"

"I needed a break," Josh said. "Anyway, I've been thinking. We could make up flyers about Fang and put them on telephone poles and in stores. Maybe the owner will see one. I can print the flyers on my computer."

"Hey, that's a terrific idea!" exclaimed Oliver.

"Yeah," said Sam.

"Then let's get to work," said Josh.

"First," said Oliver, "come over to my house so you can see Fang again. I want you to get a good look at him, so you can describe him." Oliver led his friends back to his house, upstairs, and into his bathroom. Fang was taking a sun bath. He was lying lazily under the sun lamp, his eyes closed.

"Let's see," said Josh. "Do you have a pad of paper, Oliver? I want to take some notes."

Oliver brought Josh paper and a pencil.

Josh began scribbling away. "Black body," he murmured, "yellow stripes. Dark eyes . . . dark beady eyes. I'd better say how big he is, or people might think Fang is a full-grown alligator."

"He looks like he's about two feet long," said Sam.

"Longer," said Jennifer.

"Shorter," said Matthew.

"Oliver, do you have a ruler?" asked Josh.

Oliver got a ruler from his desk and handed it to Josh.

Josh sat down on the edge of the tub and held the tip of the ruler next to Fang's nose. Fang blinked his eyes and skittered into the water.

Sam giggled. "He doesn't want to be measured."

"Wait. Let me try again," said Josh. He reached into the water, then quickly pulled his hand back. "Um, Oliver, why don't you get him?"

Oliver lifted Fang onto the block.

"Hold him there," said Josh.

"Sure. No problem." Oliver held Fang firmly. Josh placed the ruler by Fang's nose. The other end of the ruler reached near the center of his body. "One foot," said Josh. "Now for the rest of him." Josh slid the ruler down—and Fang lifted his tail up. He swished it back and forth.

"*Aughh!*" said Josh. "Make him hold still, Oliver. I have to get his tail."

"I can't. My hands are full. Hold his tail, somebody."

"I'm not holding his tail," said Sam and Matthew together.

Jennifer made a face. "Oh, all right. I'll do it." Gingerly she placed two fingers on Fang's tail. "Yuck."

"That's great, Jennifer!" said Josh. "I got it. He's twenty-three inches long."

"Okay," said Oliver. "Now you've all had a good look at Fang, so you can tell people what he looks like. Are you ready to search for his owner?"

"Yes!" they all said.

Oliver and his friends left the house. "You stay here now," Oliver told Pom-pom as he closed the front door. "This will take too long. You'll get tired."

"See you later," called Josh as he raced off to print the flyers.

"Well," Sam said to Oliver. "Where do you think we should start?"

"Over by the pond, I guess, since that's where we found Fang."

Oliver and his friends got on their bikes and rode to the pond.

"Now," said Oliver, "we'll park our bikes here, split up, and ask the people in every house if they've lost a baby alligator. Oh, and here." Oliver handed out some small white cards. "These are business cards for my pet-care service. We might as well pass them out. Maybe I'll get some new customers."

Oliver, Sam, Matthew, and Jennifer went off in different directions.

The first house Oliver came to was a small white one at the edge of the pond. He rang the bell. No one was home. Oliver left a card in the mailbox and tried the next house.

The door opened a crack and an eye peeped out.

"Hello," said Oliver. "I was wondering if you've lost a baby alligator or caiman."

The woman stared at him. "What is this, a joke?"

"No." Oliver started to explain about Fang, but decided it wasn't worth it. Obviously this woman wasn't Fang's owner.

At the house next door a small boy answered Oliver's ring. "Hi," said Oliver. "My name is Oliver Moffitt. I'm a pet-sitter, and I was wondering if you've ever owned an alligator."

The little boy nodded.

"You *have*?" cried Oliver. What luck! He could hardly believe it. "That's great, because I just found one."

"Who is it, Justin?" a voice called from inside the house.

"It's a boy, Mommy. He found Bumpy."

"What?" Justin's mother rushed to the door.

Oliver put on his best, most professional manner. "Good morning, ma'am. Oliver Moffitt, pet-care expert. No pet too tough to handle."

Justin's mother looked confused.

"Yesterday," Oliver went on, "I was sitting by the pond, and I found a baby alligator. Your son says it's his pet, Bumpy."

The woman laughed. "Justin's a little confused. Bumpy was a snake, not an alligator. We got rid of—I mean, we lost Bumpy last year."

Oliver's eyes grew wide. "You mean you had him—"

"Justin," interrupted the woman, "why don't you go watch TV?"

Justin ran off.

Oliver didn't know what to say.

"I'm sorry," said the woman. "I hope you

find the alligator's owner. Good luck." She closed the door.

For a moment Oliver stood on the front porch. How could someone just dump a perfectly nice pet? It didn't seem fair.

At the next house Angela, a classmate of Oliver's, opened the door.

"Oh, hi, Angela," said Oliver.

"Oliver Moffitt! What are you doing here?" Angela didn't like Oliver much, not since the day he had brought a tarantula to science class. The spider had escaped and crawled halfway up Angela's leg.

"I was wondering if maybe you'd lost an alligator," Oliver began.

"Are you crazy? An *alligator*? Thank you, but we have two cats and a cocker spaniel. And we used to have a chick. Nice *cuddly* pets."

"What happened to the chick?" asked Oliver.

"Oh, I got it in my Easter basket when it was little. When it got big, we let it go."

"You let it *go*? How could you do that? Do you think that chicken knew how to find food? Do you think it knew how to avoid cats? Angela, you practically—"

"Don't say it, Oliver! Look, everyone does that. My cousin got a baby bunny in her basket one year, and she let it go that summer. Animals," Angela said haughtily, "need their freedom. As an expert on pets, I'm sure you know that."

Oliver didn't reply. His face looked like a

thundercloud—angry and ready to burst. "See you," he said finally, and walked off.

No one was home at the next two houses. Oliver looked around. Across the street was a white brick house that faced the pond.

An elderly man answered Oliver's ring. "Yes?" he said.

"Hello, I'm Oliver Moffitt, pet-sitter," said Oliver. He handed the man a card. The man put on a pair of glasses and squinted at the card. "Have you by any chance ever owned an alligator or a caiman?" asked Oliver.

"Why, yes, I have," replied the old man slowly. Oliver's stomach flip-flopped. At last!

But the man continued. "About twenty years ago. My brother gave him to me as a souvenir from a trip to Florida. Cute little fellow. Had to let him go, though."

"Oh," said Oliver sadly. "Why?"

"Grew."

Oliver nodded.

"Grew like the dickens. Wanted to eat everything in sight. Couldn't keep him in the bathtub any longer."

Oliver gulped. "You know, sir, what you did wasn't very nice to the alligator."

"You mean letting him go? Oh, now, don't be so soft, young man. People do it all the time. Can't concern yourself with it."

"Oh, yes I can," thought Oliver as he turned away. "I can too."

Oliver had had more than enough searching for one day. He left a note on the handlebars of

Sam's bike, telling everyone to meet tomorrow. Then he got on his bike and pedaled away from the pond.

The last person Oliver wanted to run into was Rusty Jackson. But as he turned the corner, there was Rusty. He was carrying his box of Purple Worms souvenirs.

"Hey, Moffitt!" called Rusty.

Oliver slowed down. He parked his bike. "Are you still trying to sell that junk?" he said.

"Yeah. You know that ring the alligator chewed? I sold it to a kid for two bucks. Told him the teeth marks were from the alligator in the video." Rusty thought that was pretty funny. "That reminds me. I wanted to tell you about a phone call I made—to Pet Paradise."

"The store that sells rare pets?"

"You got it. I saw a big sign in the window that said Alligator Wanted. The guy who answered the phone was *very* interested when I mentioned Fang." Rusty smiled. "You know how much he said he'd pay for him? A hundred dollars. *One hundred smackers.* We could split it, fifty-fifty."

"Forget it," said Oliver. "No way, not on your life, absolutely not, N-O, no." He rode away from Rusty.

"Like I said, Oliver Moffitt, you'll be sorry!" Rusty shouted after him. "Really sorry!"

"You're a jerk, Rusty Jackson, you know that? A big jerk!" Oliver yelled back.

Oliver was angry. He needed some time to

think. Instead of going straight home, he rode to the school playground and sat on the swings for almost an hour. He was trying to figure out what to do about Rusty, Fang, and Fang's missing owner. He didn't come up with any answers, but at last he felt better. He rode home.

When Oliver finally parked his bike in the garage, he noticed that his mother's car was gone. "She must have had an errand to run," thought Oliver, getting out his key to let himself in. He was about to collapse on the sofa, but a horrible sight met his eyes. Oliver blinked. He blinked again.

"Oh, no!" he cried.

The living room was a shambles. A roll of paper towels had been shredded and strewn all over the floor. The edge of the sofa had been ripped and the stuffing was pouring out. There were tooth marks all over one leg of the coffee table. And Pom-pom was cowering under a chair.

"*You* didn't do this, did you?" Oliver asked him.

Pom-pom trembled with fear.

"I didn't think so." Oliver patted him, then ran upstairs. Pom-pom followed him timidly.

The bathroom door was ajar. Oliver groaned. He pushed it open and looked inside. Pom-pom slipped in after him.

There was Fang, stretched out on his block. But something was wrong. Fang was lying still, too still. And Pom-pom had put his paws up on the edge of the tub and was sniffing at him.

"Hey," said Oliver suspiciously, "why aren't you afraid of Fang?"

In answer Pom-pom lunged forward and grabbed the alligator.

"Pom-pom!" shouted Oliver. "Cut that out!"

But Pom-pom wouldn't stop. He attacked Fang, snarling fiercely. The next thing Oliver knew, Pom-pom was tearing at the alligator with his teeth—and stuffing was coming out.

It wasn't Fang at all. It was just a stuffed alligator!

The real Fang was . . . missing.

CHAPTER
5

"**P**om-pom, you're not so brave after all!" exclaimed Oliver. "Attacking a stuffed alligator." He stopped to think. "I sure wish you could talk, though. What's going on here? Fang must be around somewhere. I know he made that mess in the living room, because this alligator sure didn't."

Oliver dashed out of the bathroom and searched the rooms upstairs. He looked under beds and chairs and tables, everywhere Fang could possibly fit. Then he ran downstairs and did the same thing there. No Fang. And no more messes.

"Where on earth did he go? And where did

that stuffed alligator come from?" wondered Oliver.

Hastily he cleaned up the living room, picking up as much of the stuffing and shredded toweling as he could. Then he vacuumed the rug. He couldn't do anything about the chewed-up coffee table or the torn upholstery on the couch, but the better the room looked, the less angry his mother would be. "What am I going to tell Mom?" Oliver thought. "And how will I ever be able to pay for all this stuff?"

When he finished, Oliver got on the phone. He dialed Josh's number.

"Emergency," he said. "Can you get over here right away?"

Josh rang Oliver's doorbell exactly five minutes later.

Oliver told him what had happened. "So," he said finally, "someone or something—probably Fang—wrecked the living room. And then Fang disappeared and a fake Fang was left in his place. The stuffed alligator is our only real clue, but I'll bet I know who did it. Rusty."

Oliver told Josh about Pet Paradise and the sign. "He must have stolen Fang while I was at the playground. The only problem is, I can't prove it."

"Hmm," said Josh. "Let's comb the living room and the bathroom again. Maybe some more clues will turn up."

The boys searched every inch of the living room, but they didn't see anything unusual.

"Of course, I vacuumed," Oliver pointed out. "I hope I didn't clean away any evidence."

Josh began to protest. "Well, I had to," Oliver explained. "Mom's going to be angry enough as it is."

"Let's go search the bathroom." Josh sighed.

Upstairs, Josh examined the stuffed alligator. "Before Pom-pom attacked it, it looked exactly like Fang," said Oliver.

Josh nodded. Then he began checking every inch of the tub and Fang's block. Oliver lifted the bath mat and peered underneath. He poked in the linen closet. "Well, no clues here, I guess. . . . Hey!" he cried. "What's that?" Oliver dived for a small spot of color on the floor near the bathroom scale. "Josh! Look at this! It's a Purple Worms ring."

Josh leaped out of the tub.

"Well, well, well," said Oliver softly. "It looks like Rusty Jackson made a big mistake."

"Oliver! I'm back!" Mrs. Moffitt's voice floated up the stairs to Oliver's room.

"Oh, boy, I'm in for it now," Oliver said to Josh.

Josh nodded. "I'll leave."

"Okay. Could you find Sam and Matthew and tell them about Fang? Jennifer, too, if she's still around, but I'll bet she's already gone home. I think they should stop the search, at least for today. After all, now they're searching for the missing owner of a missing alligator. It doesn't make much sense. Also, as soon as we can,

we'll have to decide what to do about Rusty. Right now we still don't have any real proof that he's the thief.''

"OLIVER!" Mrs. Moffitt's voice sounded a lot less friendly than before.

"Uh-oh," said Oliver.

The boys went downstairs and Josh said hello and good-bye in the same breath, escaping out the front door.

"Oliver Moffitt, what is this mess?"

"What mess?" said Oliver. "I cleaned everything up."

"If this is clean, I'd hate to see what messy looks like!" Mrs. Moffitt pointed angrily at the couch. "Look at this sofa! What happened here?"

"Mom," began Oliver, "this is hard to believe. Even *I'm* not sure what happened."

"Young man. . . ."

"Honest, Mom. I came home from looking for Fang's owner and found this mess in the living room. . . . I must-have-left-the-bathroom-door-open-I'm-really-sorry-Mom," said Oliver in a rush. "But the weird part is, Fang is missing and a stuffed alligator was left in his place."

"What?"

"Yeah. I think Rusty Jackson did it, but I can't prove it—yet."

"That Rusty," said Mrs. Moffitt, clucking her tongue. "I believe I'll get on the phone and have a little chat with his mother."

"No, Mom! Please don't!" cried Oliver. "I can handle this. Give me until Friday and I promise that I'll have a home for Fang and I'll solve the mystery."

Mrs. Moffitt sighed. "All right. Just one question, Oliver. If Fang was wearing his muzzle, how did he do all this damage?"

"I really don't know, Mom. I guess I'll find out when I catch Rusty. And I will catch him. I promise."

But Oliver didn't feel as certain as he sounded. Could he really solve the mystery by Friday? What if Rusty wasn't the thief? All the signs pointed to him, but after all, Rusty wasn't the only one who could have left a Purple Worms ring behind. By now he'd probably sold them to everyone in school. The thief could be anybody.

CHAPTER
6

Sunday was not a good day for Oliver. First he got a phone call from Jennifer.

"Hi, Oliver," she said, her voice quavering.

"Jennifer? Is anything wrong?"

"Oh . . . no." Sniffle, sniffle.

"Are you sure?"

"Well, I did hear about Fang. Josh told me. That's really too bad. I guess you must be pretty worried about him—how he's missing his seventy-degree water—"

"Eighty to ninety-five," corrected Oliver.

"—and his . . . his grubs and slugs."

"Insects and raw meat."

"I mean, how many people know how to take proper care of an alligator?"

"Not many," said Oliver. "Who'd ever think an alligator needs a sun lamp?"

There was a pause at Jennifer's end. "Why, no one," she finally said. "It's—it's just like in that Purple Worms song, the one about knowing the person you love, 'Know, know, know your baby, and—' "

"Jennifer," Oliver interrupted, "excuse me, but I've really got to go. I have a lot to do. I'll see you in school tomorrow."

As soon as Oliver hung up, he called Sam.

"Hi, Oliver," she said. "I'm glad you called. I've been thinking. Josh already printed the flyers. Even though Fang's missing, I think we should post them. After all, maybe people have seen Fang. Then the flyers will help us find him *and* his owner."

"That's true," said Oliver. "Okay. Let's get everyone together. Then we can put up the flyers this afternoon."

"Great. See you."

Josh's flyer said:

FOUND

Lovable baby alligator (or caiman),
23" long, black with yellow stripes,
dark beady eyes.
Cute and pretty well-behaved.

If you are the owner, please call:
Oliver Moffitt
555-8058
23 Sutherland Avenue

Oliver and his friends posted every single flyer that afternoon. For a little while Oliver began to feel better. But not for long.

When he got back to his room, Oliver peeked into Mr. Brown's jar. "Oh, no!" he said. Mr. Brown was lying on his back on an oak leaf with his feet curled up. When Oliver poked him, he felt brittle and dry. "Please, Mr. Brown," Oliver begged, "move."

But the bug just lay there.

"Oh, great," thought Oliver. "This is just fine— *exactly* what I need. Kelly will be home tomorrow, and I'll have to tell her that Mr. Brown died."

He was still trying to figure out how he'd explain things to Kelly, when the phone rang. It was Josh. "Oliver!" he exclaimed. "I just got home from putting up the flyers. The last place I went to was Pet Paradise. And guess what?"

"What?"

"It's open on Sunday. So I went inside. Do you know why?"

"Why?"

"Because the Alligator Wanted sign wasn't in the window. It was gone."

"Oh, no."

"I wanted to see if Fang was in the store, but the owner said the alligator had already been sold. And I couldn't find out where he got the alligator from."

"Oh, no. Oh, no!"

"It doesn't look good," said Josh. "But—we

don't know for sure that the alligator was Fang. So I think we should leave the flyers up."

"All right." Oliver sighed. He hung up the phone, then stared at it for a long time. "Now, you be quiet," he said to the phone. "I've had enough bad news today."

On Monday afternoon Oliver rode slowly home from school, thinking about what he had to tell Kelly. He turned a corner and pedaled past the Helfmans' house.

Suddenly he screeched to a halt. Kelly was in her front yard.

She spotted Oliver at once. "Oliver! Oliver!" she called. "Hi! I'm home!"

Oliver's heart began to pound. He got off his bike and walked up to Kelly. "Hi, Kelly," he said.

"How's Mr. Brown?"

Oliver looked down at Kelly's eager face. "Well," he said, "he's, um—"

"When can I get him? Can I come home with you now?"

Oliver drew in a deep breath. "Kelly," he said, "I have to tell you something—something sad."

Kelly's eyes grew very wide and dark. "What?" she said.

"Kelly," Oliver began. He licked his lips. "I did everything I could for Mr. Brown, but he died. I'm really sorry. You can have his jar back, and your twenty-seven cents. Okay?"

Kelly's lower lip began to tremble. Then the

tears started to fall and she let out a howl. Mrs. Helfman ran out the front door and over to Kelly. She glanced at Oliver.

"Mommy, Mr. Brown is dead!" wailed Kelly.

"I'm sorry," said Oliver.

"Are you and Kelly talking about that bug of hers?" Mrs. Helfman asked Oliver.

"Yes," he replied. "She gave Mr. Brown to me, so I could take care of him while you were away."

"I didn't know she was going to do that."

"I'm sorry," Oliver said for the third time. "Really. I've never lost a pet before. I mean, not this way."

Oliver reached into his pants pockets and pulled out two pieces of gum, a length of string, a rubber band, and some change. He counted out twenty-seven cents and handed it to Kelly. "I didn't earn this. I'll go get the jar for you in a minute." He turned to Kelly's mother.

"You know, I wanted to tell Kelly about bugs— how they usually don't last—but I just couldn't do it. Now I wish I had." Oliver turned to go.

"Just a second," said Mrs. Helfman, putting her hand on Oliver's shoulder. She turned back to Kelly. "Sweetheart, I'm very sorry about Mr. Brown. I had no idea he meant so much to you. Would you like to go to the woods and look for another bug this weekend?"

"No!" wailed Kelly.

"Well," said her mother, "you just tell me when you're ready, and we'll get another bug then. How's that?"

"No!" cried Kelly. "I don't want another bug!"

"You don't?"

"No! I want a cat!"

"A *cat*?"

"You said when I could prove I was 'sponsible, we could get a cat. I was very 'sponsible with Mr. Brown. I fed him and took care of him, and I even found a pet-sitter for him. But now everything's ruined because *he* killed Mr. Brown!" Kelly pointed at Oliver.

"Is *that* what this is all about?" asked Mrs. Helfman. She thought for a moment. "Kelly, I'd say you've been very responsible. You made arrangements to care for your pet when your dad and I had forgotten all about him. It's not your fault—or Oliver's—that Mr. Brown died. Bugs are difficult to keep as pets."

"That's right," said Oliver, feeling better. "I'm surprised you kept him for as long as you did. That was a hard job."

Mrs. Helfman went into the house for a few seconds, came back out, and handed Oliver some money. "Here. I'd say you earned this. You were pretty responsible yourself. Thank you for being so honest with Kelly."

"No problem," replied Oliver, "but I can't take the money. I didn't do much. And Mr. Brown *did* die."

"Please," said Mrs. Helfman. "I want you to have it. You helped teach both Kelly and me a good lesson."

"Well," said Oliver, thinking about all the

money Fang had cost him, "all right. Thanks, Mrs. Helfman."

Mrs. Helfman smiled. Then she turned to Kelly. "We'll get you a kitten this week, how's that?" she said.

"Hooray!" cried Kelly, jumping up and down.

Oliver headed for his bike. "Do you want Mr. Brown's jar back, Kelly?" he asked.

"No, you can keep it."

"Okay. Thanks," called Oliver. And he rode home feeling relieved about Kelly. But he still had a big problem. Where in the world was Fang?

CHAPTER 7

On Tuesday Oliver went straight to his room after school. He waited for over an hour and the phone didn't ring once. The flyers had been up for two days and not a single person had called about Fang's owner or about Fang.

To make matters worse, Rusty had been absent from school on both Monday and Tuesday with a bad cold. So Oliver hadn't been able to ask him about Fang. He was no closer to finding a home for Fang or solving the mystery than he had been on Saturday.

"Maybe I'll go to Mr. Whitman's house," thought Oliver. "I could look at his alligators and caimans. That might cheer me up."

Oliver jumped on his bike and rode to Mr.

Whitman's funny old house. He paused in front of it and looked at the scraggly, overgrown yard and the turrets and towers that seemed to poke out in all directions. The place was huge. It had to be, Oliver supposed, in order to be a home to so many reptiles.

As Oliver stood looking at the house, Mr. Whitman stepped onto the porch and held the door open. Oliver drew in his breath when he saw who was beside Mr. Whitman. It was Jennifer! Oliver ducked behind a bush.

Something wasn't right. Why was Jennifer visiting Mr. Whitman? She hated science. She didn't even like Mr. Whitman very much. Oliver felt a tingle up his spine. . . .

He waited until Jennifer was gone. Then he waded through the tall grass and rang Mr. Whitman's bell. He heard a dog bark and heavy footsteps. Then Mr. Whitman's Santa Claus face appeared in the little window next to the door. When he saw Oliver, he grinned widely.

"Well, well! Oliver!" he boomed, opening the door. "My goodness! This certainly is a day for visitors."

"Oh," said Oliver. "I don't want to bother you—"

"No bother at all. Come right in. Your friend Jennifer was just here."

"Jennifer!" said Oliver, pretending to be surprised. "Does she . . . does she visit you often?"

"Nope. First time. Why don't you come on in?"

Mr. Whitman closed the door behind Oliver

73

and ushered him inside. Oliver wasn't sure just which room he was in, since every room on the ground floor of Mr. Whitman's house looked the same—cages and tanks from floor to ceiling. Some were big, some were huge, and each held some sort of reptile or amphibian.

Oliver saw snakes and lizards, toads and frogs, and more. There was equipment everywhere—sun lamps, water filters, air purifiers. They were all part of Mr. Whitman's experiment.

"Well, what can I do for you today, Oliver? Do you have more questions about your alligator?"

Before Oliver could answer, Mr. Whitman continued. "You know, there seems to be a run on alligators these days. Jennifer has one too. They must be pretty popular gifts."

"Since when does Jennifer have an alligator?" Oliver thought in growing suspicion.

"Mr. Whitman," said Oliver in a rush. "I just remembered something. . . . Um, I just remembered we have to memorize twenty spelling words for a test tomorrow. I'd better go. But I'll be back. Thanks anyway."

Oliver was out the door and running across the lawn by the time Mr. Whitman managed to say, "Come back soon. Thanks for dropping by."

Oliver waved awkwardly over his shoulder as he sped away. He pedaled as fast as he could all the way to his street, and then right to Josh's house. Josh, Matthew, and Sam were tossing a football around in the yard.

Oliver jumped off his bike and ran toward them. His heart was beating so fast and he was so out of breath that he had to bend over, for a few seconds before he could speak.

"You guys!" he finally gasped. "Am I ever glad I found you together!"

"Oliver, what is it?" asked Sam, looking worried.

"I think I know who has Fang—but I can't figure out why she took him."

"She?" repeated Josh.

Oliver nodded. His breathing was almost back to normal. "It's Jennifer. I got this really weird phone call from her on Sunday. She was crying, and now that I think of it, she was sort of trying to get information—like what kind of food Fang eats, and stuff."

Oliver began to frown. "Then today—just now—I was over at Mr. Whitman's house and guess who I saw leaving before I went in? Jennifer. She told Mr. Whitman she had a pet alligator. But I think she was over there trying to find out more about taking care of Fang."

"Hmm," said Matthew. "That does look pretty bad for Jennifer, but why would she want Fang?"

"Wait a minute!" said Sam suddenly. "*I* know why. Because of the Purple Worms and their new video. Jennifer will do almost *anything* to be like the Worms."

"You're right," said Oliver.

"What should we do now?" asked Josh.

"I think," replied Oliver, "that it's time to pay a little visit to Jennifer Hayes."

CHAPTER
8

Ding-dong.

Oliver stood impatiently on Jennifer's doorstep. Behind him were Josh, Sam, and Matthew. "Where is she?" said Oliver. "I was so—"

He broke off when the door opened. Jennifer stood there.

Oliver put his hands on his hips. He thought Jennifer looked a little sheepish. "Jennifer," he said sternly, "do you by any chance know where Fang is?"

"Fang?"

"You know, that cute little alligator whose owner you went looking for?"

Jennifer glanced from Oliver to Sam to Josh to Matthew and back to Oliver.

"Excuse me." Sam spoke up. "Jennifer, may I use your bathroom?"

"Oh . . . sure," replied Jennifer. "Use the one downstairs."

Sam went inside. "Thanks," she said.

"Excuse me, but I have to use the bathroom too," said Oliver.

"Me too," said Josh.

"Me too," said Matthew.

"Um . . . well, why don't you line up in the living room," Jennifer suggested nervously. "You can use the bathroom when Sam's finished."

Oliver tried his best to blush. "It's sort of an emergency," he whispered to Jennifer. "But no problem. I'll just run upstairs."

"So will we!" cried Josh and Matthew. They pushed past Jennifer.

"Hey! Stop! You can't do that!" she cried. But no one paid attention.

Oliver ran into the first bathroom he found— and there was Fang. He was lying in the tub, which was filled with about an inch of cool water. Fang looked sleepy and felt chilled. He didn't move when Oliver called his name, or even when he placed his hand on his back.

Josh and Matthew had crowded into the doorway behind Oliver. Behind them Sam and Jennifer were thundering up the stairs. "You can't do this!" Jennifer was shouting. "This is trespassing! It's against the law."

"Well, you stole Fang. Stealing's against the law too, in case you didn't know!" Oliver

shouted at Jennifer. "Look at Fang. He's half dead. And it's all your fault."

Jennifer began to cry. "I know," she sobbed. "I'm sorry. I didn't mean to do anything wrong."

"But you *did* take him," Oliver pointed out, "and you left that silly stuffed alligator in Fang's place."

Jennifer reached for a tissue and blew her nose. "You're right," she admitted, "but I hadn't planned to. See, on Saturday I got tired of searching for Fang's owner, and I thought Fang must be bored locked up by himself in your bathroom. So I got this stuffed alligator that was in our attic, and I took it to your house. I was going to give it to Fang to keep him company.

"I rang your bell, and no one answered. But the door was open. I decided it would be okay just to run upstairs for a few minutes. So I did. I gave Fang the stuffed alligator."

Jennifer sobbed and looked around at the kids. "Then I thought I'd slip the muzzle off to make him more comfortable—and the next thing I knew he had escaped. When I finally found him downstairs, he was chewing up practically everything in sight. I felt terrible."

Her tears began to fall faster. "Then I heard someone at the front door. I didn't want to get in trouble, and I didn't want Fang to get in trouble, either. So I just wrapped him up in my jacket, ran out the back door, and took him home with me."

She looked at Oliver. "I didn't mean to steal him. Honest, Oliver." By now Jennifer was crying so hard, they could hardly understand her. "Look how cute he is. He's just like the Purple Worms' alligator. I almost felt like I was one of the Worms myself. But then Fang got sick and . . . and I didn't know *what* to do. It's all a mess."

"Okay," said Oliver after a moment. "Look, the important thing is Fang. Have you given him any time to dry off since you took him? Did you get a sun lamp?"

"No, I—"

"Did you warm up his water every morning?"

"Well, sort of—"

"Jennifer," said Oliver softly, "I think Fang is really sick. We'd better get him to Mr. Whitman's right away."

For the second time that afternoon Oliver stood in front of Mr. Whitman's house. This time he was carrying Fang in a box. And this time Sam, Josh, Matthew, and Jennifer were with him.

Mr. Whitman looked surprised to see them.

"More visitors?" he boomed.

"It's an emergency," said Oliver. "There was a mix-up, and my alligator is very sick."

"Come on in."

Oliver and his friends crowded inside. Oliver opened the box, and Mr. Whitman peered in. "A bit under the weather," he said after a moment, "but nothing I can't fix. Oliver, would you be willing to leave the little fellow here for a few days?"

"No problem," he replied. "I was going to suggest that myself."

CHAPTER 9

After two days with Mr. Whitman, Fang was much better.

"I could take him back now," Oliver told Mr. Whitman in school on Thursday afternoon. "It would be okay. I have a sun lamp and everything."

"Why don't you just leave him with me? He's adjusted very nicely. I don't mind having him. Hardly know he's there."

"Well ... all right," said Oliver slowly. "If you don't mind. My mother doesn't really want him back anyway. Not after what he did to our living room. I'll just keep searching for the owner." Oliver had to admit to himself that his search looked pretty hopeless. Not one single person had called about Fang.

Oliver went home from school that afternoon feeling discouraged. He was glad Fang had a home, but he knew that Fang would be happiest with his real owner. Oliver sat down at his desk and stared at a copy of Josh's flyer about Fang. The doorbell rang.

Oliver ran downstairs. He opened the front door a crack and peered out. A big, muscular young man with curly black hair and a slick handlebar mustache was standing on the stoop. He was wearing a pair of floppy red sneakers and a suit made from cloth that looked like leopard fur.

Strangest of all was the leash in the man's hand. Oliver's eyes traveled from the handle of the leash, down, down, down—to a huge alligator wearing a jeweled collar. Oliver's jaw dropped. He opened the door the rest of the way.

"Hello," said the man. "Would you be Oliver Moffitt?"

"Y-y-yes," Oliver managed to say.

"I saw your poster in town and came here to look for Baby Archibald. That's Mimi's son." The man smiled. "This is Mimi." The man pointed to the fat, grinning alligator.

"Baby Archibald?" Oliver repeated.

"That's right. I'm Alligator Al, owner and manager of Alligator Al's Traveling Circus." Oliver didn't know what to say. He wanted to invite the man in, but he knew his mother would be very upset if he allowed another alligator into the living room. Especially one as big as Mimi.

"What's the matter? Cat got your tongue?" asked Alligator Al.

Oliver nodded.

Alligator Al grinned. "May I see the alligator you found? Dollars to doughnuts, it's Baby Archibald. We traveled through town a couple of weeks ago on our way back to Florida, and Baby Archibald escaped somewhere around here. He's a real handful," he sighed. "I've been searching ever since."

"He must be my alligator then," said Oliver. "I call him Fang. He's a handful all right. He scared Pom-pom—that's our dog—and ate part of the sofa and some towels, and chewed up the coffee table."

"Ah," said Al. He smiled approvingly. "Archibald has his mother's appetite. Just last week Mimi ate twelve pairs of socks and a clown's wig."

"I'd like to invite you in," said Oliver, "but I don't think my mother would allow Mimi in the house."

"I quite understand," said Al. "I'll just chain her up out here."

"Oh, no. That's okay. Fang—I mean Baby Archibald—isn't here anyway. I took him to stay with a friend of mine—someone who could take better care of him than I could."

"Oh," said Al. "Well, let's go. I've got my truck here."

Oliver looked outside. Parked in the Moffitts'

driveway was a big red truck. On its side, in fancy gold letters, were the words ALLIGATOR AL'S TRAVELING CIRCUS.

"I'll ride my bike," said Oliver, "and you can follow me. That way you won't have to give me a ride back after you get Baby Archibald."

So Oliver sped through town on his bike with Al and Mimi following him in the truck. The three of them gathered on Mr. Whitman's doorstep. When Mr. Whitman saw his visitors, he opened his eyes wide.

"Well, I'll be," he said.

"Hi, Mr. Whitman," said Oliver. "This is Alligator Al. . . ."

Al and Mr. Whitman shook hands.

". . . and this is Mimi. Guess what—Mimi is Fang's mother, and Alligator Al is his owner. Fang's real name is Baby Archibald."

"Well, I'll be," said Mr. Whitman again.

"They've come to get Fang."

"It's time to go to Florida for the winter," added Al.

"Just a moment," said Mr. Whitman. He went into one of the rooms, reached into a tank, and lifted out Fang. He put him into the box Oliver had brought over on Tuesday. Then he carried the box to the front door.

"Well, there you are, little fellow," said Alligator Al as he looked into the box. "This is Baby Archibald, all right. Am I ever glad to have him back! We're training him to be in an act with his mother."

At that moment Fang peeked out of the box.

When he saw Mimi, he scampered onto the porch. He climbed onto his mother's back and clung there.

"That's his first trick!" said Alligator Al. "We taught him to ride on his mommy's back!"

"Well, he looks like he's glad to be there," Oliver said.

"This is wonderful!" said Mr. Whitman. "Would you like something to eat or drink?"

"Thank you," replied Al, "but Mimi and Baby Archibald and I have a long trip ahead of us. Now that I've found Archibald, we have to hurry and catch up with the rest of the circus."

"Oh," said Oliver. He was pleased to have found Fang's owner, but he didn't want to say good-bye to the alligator.

"Well, thank you very much, Oliver Moffitt. You too, Mr. Whitman. Mimi and I are most grateful. If either of you ever decides to visit Sopchoppy, Florida, look me up. I'll give you a free ticket to my circus."

"Thanks," said Oliver and Mr. Whitman together.

Alligator Al reached into his pocket and pulled out a checkbook and a pen. He scribbled something on one of the checks, tore it off, and handed it to Oliver.

Oliver gasped when he saw it. "This—this is for. . . ."

"For all your trouble," said Al. "Baby Archibald is very important to me. I was lucky he found someone who would take such good care of him."

"But this is a lot of money. . . ." said Oliver.

"For damages."

"*Oh.*" Oliver thought quickly. The check would cover the cost of a new table and repairs to the couch, with a little money left over. "Thank you very much," he said to Al.

Al put Baby Archibald back into the box and set him on the ground. He let Mimi nuzzle him for a moment. "Well," he said, "I'll just be on my way." He loaded the two smiling alligators into the red truck.

"Good-bye!" called Oliver. "Good-bye, Fang!"

Alligator Al waved as he backed the truck into the street.

Despite himself, Oliver sighed with relief. Then he thanked Mr. Whitman again and rode home.

Back in his yard, Oliver found his friends waiting for him.

"Oliver, look!" cried Kelly Helfman. She ran to Oliver and opened a basket she was carrying. Oliver, Josh, Matthew, Jennifer, and Sam crowded around and peeked inside.

Curled up on an old sweater was a tiny, fuzzy gray kitten.

"We just got him," said Kelly, grinning broadly. "And we did a good deed too. You know who gave him to us? The Cat Lady."

Oliver smiled as he remembered the funny old woman who walked through the streets of the neighborhoods near the pond, feeding and caring for all the stray and abandoned cats.

"We saw her feeding the cats, and she said this kitten was all alone and needed a home. So we gave him one."

"Aw, he's cute," said Oliver, patting the kitten gently. "What's his name?"

"Guess," said Kelly.

"I can't."

"His name," Kelly said grandly, "is Fang."

Oliver grinned. Then he told his friends the good news about the other Fang. "So," he said, "it's a good thing we never accused Rusty. I'm sorry we ever suspected him."

"Rusty may have his bad points," said Josh, "but I guess he's not *all* bad."

"Right," agreed Oliver.

"Gosh," said Jennifer, "I'm going to miss Fang. It was fun being like the Purple Worms."

"Buy a T-shirt from Rusty," said Sam with a giggle. "Then you can at least *look* like them!"

"Here's your chance," said Josh, pointing.

Sure enough, there was Rusty walking up the block, carrying another big box. *"Ah-choo!"* he said. "Hello, hello, hello. Step right up, everyone. I've got a whole new load of Purple Worms stuff. *And* I've got an inside scoop on the Worms' next video."

"Really?" said Sam. "Is the alligator in this one too?"

"Nah." Rusty shook his head. "This one is even better. It's called *You're the Gorilla I Love.* The Purple Worms actually dance with an orangutan!"

"Ooh!" said Jennifer, her eyes glazing over in a trance.

Oliver and his friends looked at each other. "Oh, no!" they said. "Here we go again!"